For all my sisters

First published in Great Britain in 2021 and in the USA in 2022 by
Otter-Barry Books, Little Orchard, Burley Gate, Herefordshire, HR1 3QS
• www.otterbarrybooks.com

A catalogue record for this book is available from the British Library.

ISBN 978-1-91307-458-6
Illustrated with Photoshop / Digital drawing

Printed in China
1 3 5 7 9 8 6 4 2

Poems by
Rachel Rooney

Illustrations by
Milo Hartnoll

Otter-Barry BOOKS

Contents

Introduction

Not long ago, I found a poem I'd written as a young teen. It was scrawled on a scrap of lined paper and kept in a box in the attic, buried among the memorabilia: old diaries, photos, certificates and music flyers. It's a simple four-liner that I'd never thought to show anyone – and yet I'd kept it safe all these years.

I remember writing it one summer evening, having returned to my room after a mini-adventure. I don't know why, but I'd decided to climb out of the bedroom window, edge along the sloping roof tiles, and perch against the chimney stack until it grew dark. (Don't do this at home, folks.) The poem is a snapshot portrait of my younger self; an introspective girl, awed by the vastness of the universe, and feeling a sense of isolation and vulnerability within it.

Such emotions can often kick-start a poem into being, but for that to happen you need some control over these thoughts and feelings. What do I want to say here? Which words or images work hardest to make this happen? How best to arrange them on the page? Does it matter if I get it wrong? (The answer to that last question is a clear No!) For me, the process of writing poetry is where its power lies. Control and confidence grow over time and can build a kind of inner resilience.

It was the last poem I wrote as a child. And it was many years before I returned to reading or writing poetry. But thinking back, I wish I'd carried on. Poetry might have helped me navigate some of the highs and lows that every teenager experiences. And more specifically, the experiences of an undiagnosed autistic girl.

Hey, Girl! was written with that girl in mind. Together with illustrations by my son, it bridges present with past – and feels satisfyingly like a resolution.

Rachel Rooney

The sky at night is like a precious stone,
studded with flecks of silver and a pearl.
Surrounded, even though I am alone.
Covered, like an unprotected girl.

Rachel Rooney
(Age 13)

XX

Hey, girl!
You're a miracle already.
What are the odds a cluster of cells
could grow human from a mother's womb
and arrive in a bright world, blinking and blue?
That was you.

Hey, girl!
Remember, you had the power
to commando-crawl over sharp bricks,
risk unsteady steps in hard, new shoes,
turn upside-down on swings for the view.
That was you.

Hey, girl!
You're simply a sacred being-machine.
No body is perfect but you are perfectly yours.
Hold fast to this thought if others try to undo it.
I am sending this and a kiss (or two).
I was you.

Bookish

They prop open windows; let butterflies in.
And stop doors from slamming in sudden, cold wind.

They help with my balance and make me walk tall.
They'll increase my height on a chair when I'm small.

I use them to lean on when tables aren't free
and they're handy for dinners while watching TV.

They can flatten a rose to a paper keepsake
or hide the right answers in tests that I take.

Pile them like pillows at the end of the bed.
Conversation and pictures held inside my head.

Questions on a Starry Night

Is it fear or excitement,
that lub-dub in the heart?
Are cypress trees as dark as these?
Have I counted eleven stars?

Is a cosmos always busy?
Why am I dizzy and small?
Could I scale the steeple, inhabit the sky?
Or would I slip and fall?

Are all the houses safe ones?
What do they dream? And me?
I dream of Van Gogh's *Starry Night*,
then paint it from memory.

Knots

Some when tugged, like tightening
around themselves, or anchored boats.
Some come undone, unravelling.

Some as prayers, measuring hope,
remind me what I can't forget.
Others charm, charm other folk.

Some on wrists to score the flesh.
Or, tied to bars to aid escape,
take up the strain of my descent.

Some in worlds of little weight
that hold the air I wish to sing
and fastened like the gift I gave:

a pale and small balloon, its string
out of reach, and dangling.

Currency

A silver tornado flickers
       across the floorboards.

Like coins do
       for other girls
turned nothing now
       by her expert thumbs
it stills the room

and holds her rapt
in its centre
as it passes.

Worry Doll

I had a little worry doll with peg-legs made of wood.
I bound her up in woollen thread as tightly as I could.

A strip of tablecloth was cut to fix the skirt of lace.
Carefully, in felt-tip pen, I fashioned her a face.

I found a box of safety matches, emptied out the dead.
Twice I painted over it, in fire-engine red.

I laid her on a tissue bed and whispered at her ear
then slipped my secret back inside and watched it disappear

I worry for my worry doll, so once in every while
I'll slide her out again and reapply her fading smile.

Suburbia

Last summer, skirt tucked into my knickers,
I burst through my childhood.
The world turned me giddy and light.

I straddled the swing and slid on the sky;
tipped over the grass, skimming hair.
The sun was a sacrament held on the tongue.

Fences made ladders. Earth was a springboard.
Back gardens, a short cut.
Street signs pointed the way to the wood

where I cooled in the shade, went dark.
Gathered myself a damp bracken lair
and grew shyer and wild, like a fox.

Stumbling under the eye of a lamp-post,
I dragged my way homeward,
plucking at borders, lost inside earphones.

Slipped off at my front gate to wait
for a shadow to darken the hallway;
snub-nosed against frosted glass.

?

A question mark asks for an answer.
Who? Why? What? When? How? & Where?
It's a hook looking down on a full stop.
And hangs like a cloud in the air.

Blood

A stain on my sheet
the colour of rage
a proof of my heat
the pain on a page
a path that I tread
this marking of mine
a rose on my bed
the sign of the time
a rag to a bull
the mess that I made
a statement in full
and the flag I must wave.

She-Wolf

There's a bunch of us: the schoolgirl
in her glossy tights at the bus stop,
the beautician behind the window,
the attentive hairdresser, my dentist, and me.
We're all wearing our costumes.

Sometimes I choose to unzip myself.
I grow fuzz. A tail stump appears.
My teeth lengthen in their sockets.
Nails curve and harden like moons
and my skin begins to bristle.

On these nights, I swear I'm so alive
I can trace the blood pulse in the neighbour's cat
and pinpoint the metallic scent of the stars.
See me yelp and claw at the bedsheets,
straining to keep pace with the pack.

Mask

My mask is made of flesh-tone skin
so thin it almost isn't there.

And in it, seven seamless holes
each measured up for ease of wear.

Most days I fix it to my face
before I'll open my front door.

Nobody knows I'm wearing it.
Or it wears me – I'm never sure.

It's handy for the banter at a party.
It can smile and frown.

Remains in place with nods and shakes
and if I'm looking up or down.

On coming home, I'll peel it off
and hang my gossamer disguise

back on its hook. Then look to see
myself inside my mirrored eyes.

Perspective

When I say spectrum, I mean to say
it's not a rainbow arc with pot of gold
but viewed from above, an entirety.
It's a hole, a halo, a hoop to jump,
or the scaffolding that underpins
this thought in air. A circle
of light split by droplets of water.

When viewed from above, a rainbow appears
as a complete circle.

Break-time

Your mouth moves in synchronicity
with sounds I can hear,
some of which are recognisable,
like *partyinvite* and *latestgossip*.
And somewhere deep inside you,
invisible strings are being pulled
that make your eyes swivel,
shoulders rise, palms jerk upwards.

But even though I am holding
what I hope is an understanding half-smile
and feel satisfied with the tilt of my head,
I'm thinking about that wasp in the window,
trapped amongst the stationery.
The way it alternates between
resigned torpor and active despair,
the tap of its wing against glass.

Five-Fingered Salute

That age-old trick you fall for every time:
the playground one where they extend
an empty hand and watch you take the bait.
You always dare to shake on it, agree
to disagree, make up or call it quits.

Before you get a grip, they'll whip it back
tack thumb to nose, splay nostrils wide
and waggle four fat fingers in the air.
You're left dangling while they roll their eyes.
But tell me this, who looks the stupidest?

Yawn

Remember when yawning was a thing? It started with
some kids in the year above, but yawns are contagious
and soon loads of us were at it. We became obsessed
with perfecting our techniques. We'd yawn through
registration and assembly, along corridors at break
time and later on in detention. It became an urgent
and competitive art. We'd take selfies, upload videos
of ourselves yawning to music. Back home, in our
bedrooms, we synchronised with mates on TikTok.
Extreme yawning, we called it. Can't quite believe it
now, but I still remember how good it felt: that fuzzy feel
below the earlobes, the widening jaw and that hollow
growing in the throat. Back then, I gulped down air like
I couldn't get enough of it. How I loved the chin jut, the
satisfying click when I surfed a lucky double, that
gurning as I peaked before releasing those breathy
vowels. Yes, yawning was moist-eyed bliss. One
lunchtime, mid-chew and goaded on by others, I braved
a no-hander. Even made it my avatar. Imagine that!
You'd never think yawning would catch on like it did.
I guess we were all bored back then.

Punctuation

Full Stop ended it.

Comma just went on, and on, and on.

Semicolon and I connected; we're just friends.

Ellipsis had something missing…

Brackets (I'd forgotten about them).

Apostrophe was somebody else's.

Exclamation Mark – No Way!

Could Question Mark be the one?

Doppelgänger

She's trying to pretend she isn't there.
Put in her place a girl who is the spit
of someone she once knew, who even wears
a pair of shoes that match. They seem to fit
her feet although they pinch a little tight.
She can recite her full name and if pressed
recalls her date of birth. But late at night
it feels as if she's cheated in a test.

They keep a smiling snapshot on the shelf.
Her wanted face from last year's holiday.
It looks like her but now she's someone else.
And she's not sure it was her anyway.

64 Squares

I'll never understand the rules of chess
or boys. I only know the word *checkmate*.
Perhaps that's why my love-life is a mess.

I haven't learnt the moves, it's all a guess.
My instinct is to play my bishop straight.
I'll never understand the rules of chess.

I've had beginner's luck, though I confess
my strategies are weak; I don't notate.
Perhaps that's why my love-life is a mess.

I know a Kasparov – but I digress.
I send my queen towards her captured fate.
I'll never understand the rules of chess.

A game? A sport? To me, it's simply stress.
I'd rather Scrabble or Articulate.
Perhaps that's why my love-life is a mess.

I gently tip my tired king to rest
and stop the clock. I'm choosing not to date.
I'll never understand the rules of chess.
Perhaps that's why my love-life is a mess.

Seven Dwarves

One had anger issues
and he blamed them all on me.

One stayed in his bedroom
so we met infrequently.

One was always grinning
yet he couldn't tell a joke.

One was word-allergic.
Kept on sneezing when I spoke.

One seemed keen. He flirted
but he failed to make a pass.

One looked cute (and stupid).
He got worse when smoking grass.

One believed in healing
though he never wrote a note.

Now I'm lying in a glass box
with an apple down my throat.

The Art of Deception

Deception is an art I've come to learn.
Like webs that garden spiders carefully weave
it takes a little effort, and in turn
an unsuspecting fly that might believe.

The yarn you spin must always be secure.
The words rehearsed. If using alibis
it helps to fix them first. And do ensure
misleading truths are tied in with the lies.

The body language needs to be relaxed.
Uncross the legs, reveal an open palm.
Maintain unblinking eye-to-eye contact.
A reassuring hand upon an arm.

I know all this. Yet I identify
not with the artful spider, but the fly.

truth   truth   truth truth truth
truth   truth   truth
truth   truth   truth
truth   truth   truth truth truth
truth   truth   truth
truth   truth   truth
truth truth truth   truth   truth truth truth

lies lies lies   lies lies lies   lies   lies   lies lies lies   lies   lies
         lies   lies   lies   lies   lies   lies   lies   lies
         lies   lies   lies   lies   lies   lies   lies   lies
         lies   lies lies lies   lies   lies   lies   lies lies lies
         lies   lies   lies   lies   lies   lies   lies   lies
         lies   lies   lies   lies   lies   lies   lies   lies
         lies   lies   lies   lies lies lies   lies   lies   lies

Message

Hold me to the mirror light
and make my meaning clear.
The world reverses left to right,
when I am there, not here.

Behave

I've learnt the way of strangers,
dangers in the dark,
games like patience, solitaire,
and words like patriarch.

I know my hiding places,
shoe size, weight and height,
the long way round, the short-cut,
a wrong think from a right.

I've memorised novenas,
all the school rules, lyrics. Yet
the reason for this vigilance
is harder to forget.

Satyr

I knew he'd feet; I'd seen him walk
though not imagined them before.

His boots were larger, soft-soled, silent;
hoof and print wedged in their hide.

I'd signs, of course; high steps,
steep hills, the way he took offence

when I cooled porridge, warmed my palms.
That, and the whistling down the wind.

A satyr is a mythical creature: half man, half beast.
This poem is based on one of Aesop's Fables,
The Satyr and the Traveller.

Bumper Book of Myths

Once, I kept a *Bumper Book of Myths*
beneath my quilt. I read them to believe.
Inside the cover, claiming ownership,
I wrote my signature but didn't leave
it there. Added on my home address
including *England, Britain, Europe, Earth,
The Universe*. I did it to impress
and in the hope that I might venture further
than my postcode, with my gods.
Under their protection, I could learn
to fight my battles. Nothing would be lost;
I'd return and they would be returned.

I used my special, blue handwriting pen.
Yes, everything was easier back then.

Cool, Dark Place

Take emotion when it's fresh and raw;
as it hits you in the face
like a dog's lick, like a fist on jaw.
Gather it and bottle it at source
and store in a cool, dark place.

Leave it there, preserved upon a shelf
for your return. When faint despair
reminds you that you once felt more,
uncork the smelling salt of self.
Then nose to rim, inhale its air.

Still the Wind

First, she built a house of straw.
Thatched the roof and wove the door.
Chaff, her mattress. Grain, her floor.
Still, the wind blew hard.

Next, she fashioned one from wood.
Propped it up as best she could.
Plugged the gaps with sticks and mud.
Still, the wind blew hard.

Found a stash of granite stone.
Bricked herself inside, alone.
No one heard her call it home.
Still, the wind blows hard.

Absence

Red: it's overrated. See that token
red on a single stem, that
redness of me waiting like a letterbox.

It's too easy.

Blue is foolish.
Blueness: I can dive right into it. Yes,
blue's an invite; it's the touch of tiles in a pool.

Don't do it.

Yellow's hell. Avoid it.
Yellowness is madness.
Yellow. Break it down and it's the sound it makes.

I won't enter it.

Greenness: it isn't me.
Green is someone else's scent and
green's their friends, fingers, mould.

Best keep away from it.

White? Now, that's more like it.
White's an absence. A blank fantasy.
Whiteness is wafer-paper sweetness.

Like the black ink I can almost taste.

Ghosted

It began with the losing of names:
the search, the giving in
to *thingamajig* and *whatsherface*.
She gave up answering.

Places she'd been came next.
The trace of an unmarked map
had led her down a one-way street.
There was no turning back.

Then that trick with the mirror:
the gaze at nothing at all
but the pendulum swing, the glassy stare
of an old-fashioned clock in the hall.

Last thing left was her breath
mouthed in an empty ear.
As the tide takes a shell from a shore,
she simply disappeared.

Some

love turns light
turns heads turns
take turns tables
round turns tide
turns fake turns
milk turns dark
turns cheek turns
fight turns heel
turns tail turns
leaf turns light

Moon Time

Old Moon warns us to be wise.
Snow Moon stirs the heavy skies.
And a Sap Moon slowly rises.

Egg Moon nestles in our palm.
Milk Moon brings the blossom's balm.
And a Rose Moon shows its charm.

Hay Moon lines the cattle shed.
Grain Moon offers broth and bread.
And a Harvest Moon turns red.

Blood Moon tugs the flesh from bone.
Frost Moon hardens soil to stone.
Then a Cold Moon takes us home.

Yew

Before, a redwing left a berried branch
and carried off the fruit that tasted sweet.

Afterwards, she followed in its wake,
trod in a bitter seed beneath her feet.

Before, a sapling aged into a tree
and cast a shadow on the sacred ground.

Afterwards, she gathered from its leaves
a poison, and a canker cure she'd found.

Before, the sapwood hid its flex and bend
and heartwood hid the strength it held below.

Afterwards, she dreamt of battle, love;
prepared herself a firm and steady bow.

Before all this she waited for the dark
to turn the evergreen a blackish hue

and watched the passing winter moon alight
within the branches of an Irish Yew.

If Hope Could Speak

Written for and with Chalkhill Unit

Uncertainty breathes out like fog.
It clouds the path I follow.
It sounds like a running engine
or a volcano ready to blow.

It sits alone in a darkened room.
It ticks like a clock in the night.
It is a minefield in the mind.
A blind-spot in my sight.

It clings like a cobweb to my face.
It grabs and suffocates.
It's colder than a snowstorm
or a murderer lying in wait.

But hope is wind that blows my hair
as I start the long walk ahead.
It's watching a sun set over a hill.
A sunrise seen from my bed.

It's having a goal. A leap of faith.
An unopened parachute.
A lifeguard diving in the sea.
A super-power suit.

It tastes like honeysuckle.
It is the language of birds.
If hope could speak I'd write it down
and fill the page with words.

Battle Call

I want to find the voice to speak the words
I want to shape the air and let them sing
I want to know the weightlessness of birds
I want to feel that lift beneath the wing

I want to keep those promises I made
I want to meet the girl that I once knew
I want to prove to her I'm not afraid
I want to scale the summit for the view

I want to learn the secrets of the sun
I want to brave the hailstones as they fall
I want to do all this. And when I'm done
I want the world to hear my battle call

Barrier

BARRIERBARRIERBARRIER
BARRIERBARRIERBARRIER
BARRIERBARRIERBARRIER
BARRIERFREEDOM**BARRIER**
BARRIERBARRIERBARRIER
BARRIERBARRIERBARRIER
BARRIERBARRIERBARRIER

BARRIERBARRIERBARRIER
BARRIERBARRIERBARRIER
BARRIERBARRIERBARRIER
BARRIER   *FREEDOM***BARRIER**
BARRIERBARRIERBARRIER
BARRIERBARRIERBARRIER
BARRIERBARRIERBARRIER

BARRIERBARRIERBARRIER
BARRIERBARRIERBARRIER
BARRIERBARRIERBARRIER
BARRIER   BARRIER   **FREEDOM**
BARRIERBARRIERBARRIER
BARRIERBARRIERBARRIER
BARRIERBARRIERBARRIER

Freedom

She runs barefoot down the street,
ignoring words that warn No Entry.
Dances to her own tune. When she
sings, it's from another hymn sheet.

Reads the book from a different page.
Recites the rules that she has written.
Digs a hole that she might fit in.
Picks at the lock of a songbird cage.

Marches to the sound of her own drum.
Skips a beat. Beats out a skip.
Won't be held in your palm or grip.
Or under anybody else's thumb.

Can't be grounded. She refuses
to remain behind the lines.
Looking back, I saw the signs.
She must do whatever she chooses.

Nightfall

night falls waves
break tide turns

earth quakes light
wanes mood swings

heart aches tears
sting blood cools

path bends words
stop poem ends

The Definite Article

      On this island there are no definites;
visitors don't find *the* safest way home,
only safer ways
because they haven't got *the* book,
only a book to guide them
around an island so large
even elephants would get lost here
without a map.

      On this island everything is all
some forest, some sky, some rain,
with occasional sightings of others
falling to their knees in mud.
Not *the* mud.

      On this island there is no dog.
No path.
No flashlight.
No definite boat.

Idea

My head is kinda empty
like a bucket with a hole,
or a vault that stored the money
that a nifty burglar stole.

It's as blank as copy paper,
morning snow upon the lawn
or the untouched souls of babies
seconds after they've been born.

It is hollow, like a blown egg shell,
a bubble, or a drum.
It's like waiting at a bus-stop
for a bus that doesn't come.

I've racked my brain for ages.
There is nothing to be said.
The only sound is silence
and it echoes round my head.

If thoughts were water, there would be
a drought between my ears.
Maybe I'll write a poem
about having no ideas.

Songbird

A feeling becomes a thought.
So I feel it and I think it.

A thought becomes a word.
So I think it and I name it.

A word becomes a poem.
So I name it and I sing to it.

A poem becomes a bird.
So I sing to it and I tame it.

Place

Inside my head is a factory
where information jiggles along a conveyor belt.
Quick hands pick and sort, before
machines filter, churn, can and label.

Inside my head is a marketplace
where the traders jostle to offer their opinions.
Everything's for sale, though I try to avoid
being short-changed by the bustle and the noise.

Inside my head is a hospital
where wounds are tended and ailments examined.
Behind closed curtains, quiet deaths may occur.
But prayers are recited and minor miracles performed.

Inside my head is a playground
where thought grows dizzy on roundabouts
and arcs triumphantly from swings. The world blurs
to nothing but gut feeling and the sensation of self.

Inside my head is a walled garden
where leaf and shade claim ownership of the day.
A small pond breathes in deep sunshine. I enter through
a tall gate which is sometimes, but not always, locked.

No Man's Land

Each morning I exit the back gate into No Man's Land
where decay and growth carry on regardless.
Here, the tub of rainwater dances with acrobatic life,
a bee hums its aria from a primrose chamber,
blackberry bushes drop their jewels like thieves
and shy birds gossip and stir in the ivy.

I'll sit by the tracks of an invisible fox, slide my eyes
up its flattened path to the viaduct brick
and wait for flashes of train-glass in leaf-gap.

Imagine: sunlight striking a passenger as she squints
down on a destination where anything is possible.

Reflux

This poem cannot be stolen.
I have eaten it
and left you the husk of words.
Each syllable, every gap between
has turned a tongue-rolled morsel
I followed down with milk.

This poem cannot be destroyed
by shredding or by fire.
Even now, as you are reading
it is waiting inside me,
like a bulimic's trick,
for an empty white room and a pencil.

Table Poem

It begins with the word Table.
The image of a white tablecloth smoothed flat across.
The placing of weighted objects carefully on top.

Now, let me impress you with my trick.
The one where I deftly whip away the linen
to find that

      the magnifying glass   the butter dish

        the stained chopping board

remain exactly as I left them.

Get Over It

Don't wind back the clocks to replay the time.
It is what it is, a repetitive crime.
Things I have thought about things I have done.
All the thinking.
The thinking.
The thinking.

Don't water it down to a smile or a shrug;
all that pacing around in the trench I had dug.
Something unfinished. A thought I'd begun.
All the thinking.
The thinking.
The thinking.

No need to explain, though I'll give it a try;
this pleasure, this pain and the places I lie;
In a hole – in a thought – in a poem for one.
All the thinking.
The thinking.
The thinking.

Shadows

A walk in the heavy sun
       to step through the ash trees
              splashed across the flat grass;
                     to tread over the ends of a picnic
and merge with running dogs;
       to watch cyclists lap past me,
              flatten themselves in my path.
And to turn my back on it, pause, admire a longer self
       cast on the steps and to climb, lighter now,
              into this thin dark.

Label

The trick, she thought, is not to trap it
nor to pin it to a board,
extend its wings and label it.

It's better left to wrestle free.
You see, to watch it flex the air, remain
unnamed, won't work against it.

Advice from a Caterpillar

When I was egg, I too, clung onto leaf
in shaded safety, hidden underside.
And fastened by a pinprick of belief
I dared to dream I was a butterfly.

A hunger hatched. I ate the home I knew
then inched along the disappearing green.
In shedding every skin that I outgrew,
became a hundred times the size I'd been.

And now I'm spinning silk to fix my spot.
Outside remains. Inside I'm changing things.
This caterpillar's planning on the lot:
proboscis and antennae, four bright wings.

So keep on clinging on, my ovoid one.
For who you are has only just begun.

Girl to Woman

Think of a tight-petalled bud
   Now the scented face of a flower
Think of the drizzle in mud
   Now blasted by song from the shower

Think of a second-hand tick
   Now the reach of a golden hour
Think of foundations of brick
   Now the dizzying height of a tower

Think of a girl reading this
   Now the wishes that you would allow her
Think metamorphosis
   Think girl to woman power

That's All, Folks!

You pass another roadside boulder,
three-armed cactus, tuft of grass,
more puffy clouds, each one eclipsed
by the same familiar wide-eyed crow.
And then it clicks.
You're going no place fast.
It's just a simple animation trick.
So please remember this:
be sure to keep your face in profile,
act as if you're heading somewhere,
and give your little legs a scissor-kick.
Life is like a *Looney Tune*;
the background is on loop. It sets the pace
and you are soon to meet a canyon cliff.
From previous experience I've found

it helps to pedal air and not look down.

Download

I switch off the lamp
and settle with the day;

the constellation of dark hours,
the small bursts of sunshine.

I've put it to bed like a row
or the last line written in a poem.

Outside, a siren fades into silence.
Inside, I am downloading the stars.

Blessings

May you wake with the enthusiasm of a puppy in a leaf-pile.

May you find your mobile charged at full power.

May every radio station play the tune you need to hear.

May the answers in your head match the questions you're asked

May you notice the hint of colour in a rain cloud.

May corridors become friendship tunnels.

May dinnertime pass without the start of an argument.

May you surprise yourself with your own private bravery.

May the darkness highlight one golden moment from today.

May you fall asleep as leaves rock gently from their trees.

Credit

At the end of the movie she walks a dirt track,
disappears in a heat-haze without looking back.

The theme tune fades in (*Ecstasy of Gold*).
We wait in our seats for the credits to roll.

The truth is revealing. Like everyone else,
the actress who played her was playing herself.

About the Poet

RACHEL ROONEY is one of the most admired poets writing for children and young adults today. She worked as a teacher of children with additional needs while bringing up her own three sons. She continues to take a close interest in issues around mental health, particularly for girls and women. She is the author of *The Language of Cat*, winner of the CLiPPA Award in 2011, *My Life as a Goldfish* and *A Kid in My Class*, both shortlisted for the CLiPPA.
A Kid in My Class also won the North Somerset Teachers' Book Award.
Rachel Rooney lives in Brighton.

About the Illustrator

MILO HARTNOLL is an autistic artist who makes work about internet culture, digital aesthetic and new media communication. He founded the art collective Cane-Yo. And sometimes he draws pictures.

Instagram: @milohartnoll
Twitter: @milohartnoll

With thanks to

Janetta Otter-Barry and her team
for publishing my work over the years

The students at Limpsfield Grange School
for their enthusiasm and insights

Arts Council England for their support
with my Autism & Poetry project

Susannah Herbert for her sound advice and humour

Allie Rogers for being a trusted first reader of my poems

My agent, Caroline Walsh, for her patience

Supported using public funding by
**ARTS COUNCIL
ENGLAND**